Bess
and the
Sphinx

Bess
and the
Sphinx

by Elizabeth Coatsworth

Illustrations by Bernice Loewenstein

THE MACMILLAN COMPANY, NEW YORK
COLLIER-MACMILLAN LIMITED, LONDON

An earlier version of the chapter "The Scarlet Jacket"
appeared in *Trails for Juniors* in August, 1948.
A version of the chapter "The Desert People" appeared in *Story Parade*
in September, 1948, under the title "The Scarf."

Dedicated to the Family,
and
especially to Bob,
always loved and loving

Contents

1 *Old Bear*

GRANDMA sat by the window in her big chair upholstered in black leather. The folds of her long skirt and her tight basque were as black as the leather and filled all the big chair. If Bob and Bess had looked up from the carpet beyond her feet, they could have seen, above the blackness, her handsome face with its eyes closed, her coil of white hair held up by a silver comb, and the narrow Venetian lace turned over the top of her high black collar.

But neither Bob nor Bess looked up. To them both and to Grandma too, in her chair, she was

I

a bear asleep in a hollow tree, and the children were picking strawberries from the carpet—which of course wasn't a carpet—and putting them into invisible baskets, always coming nearer and nearer to the tree from which came the loud snores of the sleeping bear.

Papa and Mama were on the other side of the room, and Papa was discussing something with Mama, who sat listening quietly with her forget-me-not blue eyes on the children. But Bob and Bess didn't know anyone else was in the room. They were alone in a dark wood. Nearer they drew to the hollow tree, reassured by the bear's deep snores.

"Oh, look, there are a lot of berries here, Bess," said Bob, who was two years older, crawling closer to the danger.

"My basket is almost full," bleated Bess, crawling nearer too, almost convinced that this time the bear would never wake up.

But just at that moment, the bear stopped snoring and sprang at them with a growl. Bob began rolling away as fast as he could roll, but Bess

3

sprang wildly to her feet, tripped, and fell, howling.

"Bess, stop that racket!" exclaimed Papa, who was always disturbed by sudden loud noises.

"They were playing Old Bear," explained Mama quickly.

"Then let her be more quiet about it," said Papa, but already his voice had lost its crossness.

"Do read to them," he added to Grandma, who was once more seated in her big chair. "I'm discussing plans for the summer."

Quiet was restored. Bess, a plump child with dark hair in a bang, dark eyes under arching brows, and a surprised-looking mouth that could at times look obstinate, climbed in Grandma's lap. Grandma, saying nothing, wiped away the silent tears that always came when Bess was scolded, hard as she tried to stop them. Bob, fair-haired with dancing gray-blue eyes, stood leaning against one of the padded arms of the chair. No one except Mama thought Bess was pretty, but everyone said how handsome Bob was, and Bess was the first to admire him.

Now Grandma reached for the copy of the children's Bible. She read many other books to the children—*Alice in Wonderland* and *Black Beauty* and *Toutou's Merry Winter*—but she preferred to read Bible stories, and she herself liked the exciting ones best. Slowly she opened the heavy cover and began to turn the pages, now and then giving her forefinger a little lick which made the pages turn more easily, an old-fashioned habit which Bess hated. But of course Bess never said anything. Now in the circle of Grandma's arm she was allowed to choose a story.

"Moses in the bulrushes and the Egyptian princess," decided Bess.

"Yes," added Bob, from his side of the chair, "and all the snake part and the plagues, too."

"No," said Bess. "Just how his mother hid the baby and how the princess found him."

Grandma began to read in a slow, rather monotonous voice, which was the way the children liked stories to be read.

The tale went on, and no one noticed that Papa and Mama had stopped talking and were listening too. When the princess called Moses's sister and told her that she was to be in charge of bringing up the baby, Bess clapped her hands in satisfaction, and perhaps to remind Grandma that she wasn't to go on to the sad parts.

"How would you like to go to Egypt too, children, and see the Nile, and palm trees and camels?" Papa suddenly asked from across the room.

"And the Egyptian princess?" Bess wanted to know.

Papa never laughed and seldom smiled, but he was often amused, and her question amused him now.

"I don't know that the princess is still around," he said. "But if she is, we'll see her. I've been telling Mama that I'd like to go abroad for seven or eight months while it won't make too much difference to your schooling. Three months of it will be vacation time anyway, and you two can easily make up the schoolwork. You'll learn more traveling than you ever could at school, and have lots more fun."

"I'll go!" said Bob, "but who'll take care of the grain elevator, Papa?"

"I have a good foreman who can manage," said Papa, "and most of the Great Lakes shipments to Buffalo are arranged for at least a year ahead. Before we know it, 1900 will be knocking at the door, and I think we should all see something of the world before *that* happens. Don't you think so, Mother?" he added, turning to Grandma.

"I always like a trip," said Grandma. "I don't see anything to prevent, if you want to go."

Bess felt a little frightened, even on Grandma's broad lap. She looked at Mama, and Mama was smiling back at her. "You'll like it," said Mama. Mama always made things right for everybody. If Mama ever wanted anything herself, she didn't say so. She wanted what Papa wanted, and then, somehow, everyone else wanted it too.

With very little fuss, the family packed and got ready. Before sailing they stayed with Great-uncle Tom and Great-aunt Jenny just outside New York City. The morning they were off, Grandma said grace at breakfast and added something about the

7

perils of the deep, which Bess didn't understand. Grandma had a new black dress and coat. She always wore black except for best, when she wore lavender. Papa looked nice, and Mama was wearing a dashing navy blue suit and a light blue hat with a sea gull's wing on it.

"It isn't a real wing," she assured Bess. "I wouldn't wear one. This is just made of white chicken feathers." Mama looked very pretty and very happy. She may have agreed to go so quickly to please Papa, but anyone could see, just to look at her, that she loved to travel too.

And so they all embarked on the twenty-third of May, 1898, with Bess holding firmly to a pleat of Mama's sweeping skirt, so as not to be lost in the crowd. She was frightened by all the noise and confusion, and when finally the stewards banged on their trays to send visitors ashore and the liner gave horrible hoots, she flung herself on Papa for protection.

"Don't knock me down, Bess," he said, patting her shoulder. "It's all right. Our boat's just saying

8

good-bye to all the other boats, because it won't be seeing them for a long time."

Bess enjoyed the voyage. Later, England didn't seem very different from home, except that in England Bess learned about art galleries. The family were earnest sightseers.

In Germany Bob and Bess loved the trip up the Rhine and the rock where the beautiful Lorelei once sat, combing her golden hair and singing to lure the passing sailors to destruction.

In Switzerland they got up very early one morning and went to the top of a mountain. When the sun rose, the clouds were below them.

"Now you know what birds see," said Papa, and Bess afterward often thought about those clouds in a rosy carpet spread at her feet.

The next time Bess went high, she didn't have such a nice time. Grandma stayed in Naples, but Papa, Mama, Bob, and Bess went to the top of Vesuvius. On the way down Bob said, "Bet I can beat you, slowpoke!" Bess knew of course that he could. He was a boy, wasn't he? and two years older? But she was always so pleased when he paid attention to her that she began to gallop obediently down the steep mountainside, her short black-stockinged legs taking flying leaps she didn't know they were capable of. But a minute later she lost her balance with a shriek and fell sprawling. Bob came back at once to set her on her feet, and Papa and Mama hurried down to her and wiped away her tears, but neither they nor her tears could get the dreadful cinder out of her eye.

It took Grandma in Naples to do that.

"I see it, but you must hold steady, Bess, if you want it out."

Finally out the horrid thing came on the stiff corner of one of Grandma's plain, very white handkerchiefs, and Bess, her troubles over, could look at the great black speck which for an awful hour had been part of her.

"Cheer up, Bess," said Papa. "Day after tomorrow we sail for Egypt."

Bess forgot the old cinder.

"Will we see the Nile and palm trees and camels?" asked Bess. She had a good memory. "And an Egyptian princess?" she added.

"I can't promise a princess," said Papa. "But of course you can count on seeing the Sphinx."

Old Bear

In the hollow tree
(Darkness hidden in darkness)
  Sleeps the bear.

The strawberries grow
Red and ripe in the woods.
  Pick, if you dare!

Silently, cautiously,
Where the plants show thick
  The children creep.

Their wicker baskets
Are almost filled.
  Old Bear is asleep.

2 *The Countess and Cairo*

IT WAS Christmas Day in Cairo, not the kind of place for Santa Claus at all. Instead of snow there was dust swirling along the streets, and instead of church steeples there were tall minarets against the sky. Mosquitoes hid in the folds of the curtains at the pension windows, and when Bess looked out she saw water carriers with dripping skins slung over their ragged shoulders, running from door to door, and there were women going to market with black veils hiding their faces except for their dark eyes, and boys whacking their donkeys ahead of them down the narrow streets.

14

"Oh dear!" sighed Bess. "I'm sure Santa Claus won't find us here."

She ran to the foot of her brass bed where her stocking had been tied the night before, since of course there was no fireplace in the room.

But now there was no stocking either. Bess went to the window and looked out, to hide her tears.

"My stocking's gone too," said Bob from his bed.

"It's too far and too hot for Santa Claus to bring his reindeer," Bess said, trying to find excuses for Santa Claus. "But I wish he'd used donkeys. Mama was wrong. She said it wouldn't matter to Santa Claus *where* we were."

At thinking of what Mama had said and of all her hopes, Bess's voice broke, and after it had once broken, the sobs began to come thick and fast. As usual she couldn't find her handkerchief.

"You big crybaby," Bob snorted, half in pity. "Look, here's something in my bed. Why, Santa Claus must have hidden the stockings under my sheet while I was asleep!"

Bob quickly pulled out two black stockings filled with various wonderful knobs and bumps.

15

Bess thought, what a funny thing for Santa Claus to do. She looked at Bob a little suspiciously, but she was a very believing child.

"I think he was *mean*," said Bob.

"No, he was just fooling," cried loyal Bess. "He didn't know it would make me cry."

"Here's your stocking," went on Bob, handing one to her. Her suspicions were gone as quickly as they had come.

16

"Thank you, Bob," she said. "Have you a hanky?"

The chief present for Bess was a rather peculiar doll. It was dark and had curly hair with a head-dress of real feathers. It didn't have any clothes except for its headdress and some brightly colored cloth feathers about its middle, and a necklace of beads.

Later at breakfast Mama explained that the doll was a Fiji Islander. It made Bess feel rather funny. She had been hoping for a baby doll. She had been in Europe now for months without any doll to tell things to, and it would seem strange to tell things to an almost bare-naked Fiji Islander. But a doll is a doll.

"What will you call her?" Mama asked.

"I think it's a him," said Papa.

Grandma looked at the doll through her gold spectacles. "I think you're right, Thomas," she said to Papa. "You might call him Melchizedek."

"Call him Ben," suggested Bob.

The Old Testament was wonderful, Bess

thought, but not to name dolls after. She liked Bob's suggestion better.

As the day went on Bess found that Ben really was a comfort. Nestled in her arm, he felt better than nothing, and she didn't have to look at him. She could show him things and tell him things, too.

In the middle of the morning a very nice thing happened. A Polish count and countess were much the most exciting people at the pension, and had a whole wing to themselves, and usually ate their meals served in their rooms. They were young, and he was very handsome, and she had beautiful curly lashes and veils that floated from her wonderful hats.

This morning, when the count and countess came back from their usual drive, Bob and Bess were playing outdoors. As usual the count helped the countess down the carriage step and the countess smiled at the children, but today something different happened.

"Don't go away, children," she said in a pretty, foreign voice. "I have something for you."

It was the first time she had spoken to them.

A few minutes later they heard her voice calling. She was standing between the curtains of an upstairs window, looking, Bess thought, like a fairy princess. She smiled at them again.

Then she began tossing out candies wrapped in colored papers. Some of the papers were pink, some blue, some yellow. They fell like flowers everywhere. Bess stood staring. Mama didn't allow them to have much candy because she thought it wasn't good for them. Certainly no countess had ever tossed candy to them before. It was like a dream. Bob was picking up the sweets as they fell, but Bess still stood staring like an owl.

"But, gather them, gather them, little foolish!" the countess called. "See, big brother knows what to do with candy!"

The countess turned away from the window, breaking the enchantment, and then Bess picked up the few candies still left on the grass.

Because it was Christmas Day, the English couple who ran the pension served duck for dinner

and ice cream and chocolate cake and all kinds of good things, and for once the count and countess ate with the rest of the guests at the long pension table.

Under the countess's eyes Bess was especially careful to eat politely and never to give anything on her plate even the littlest push with her finger. But grownups take a long, long time to eat. Bess's feet didn't touch the floor, and sitting still grew harder and harder. Because it was Christmas Day, Mama had allowed her to keep Ben on her lap, out of sight. For a while he was a comfort to her, but still the chair grew harder and harder.

Like many restaurant chairs at that time, the back of Bess's was made of two curves of wood, one inside the other. She pushed against hers and found that she could slip her rear through the space made by the inner loop. It was a tight squeeze but rather exciting. She let go Ben and put her hands against the table and cautiously pushed herself through a little farther. She caught the countess's eye, and that lovely lady gave her a little smile.

21

Spurred on by the look, Bess pushed still farther. But oh! she pushed too far! She was not like Bob who knew just how to do things.

The chair lost its balance. For a dreadful moment it teetered, while Bess strove frantically to save herself. But she could not.

In silence, with an awful feeling of despair, she toppled over backward. Pinned in her ignominious position in the loop of chair back, she was borne crashing to the floor. Ben flew one way, the dishes rattled, and the countess gave a small, airy scream.

Bess's feet still stuck up straight in the air, and her hands and head too, gathered together into a bunch by her position. She struggled feebly, but she was a prisoner. Someone began to laugh, and the laugh spread from one to another down the table. All the pension guests were laughing, laughing at Bess, like a June bug waving her feet in the air.

It was Papa who, as soon as he had recovered from his first surprise, jumped up and rescued her.

22

But Ben could not be rescued. His head, with its headdress of bright feathers, was broken and lay a foot away from his brown body. Bess picked up the pieces. They were all that was left of her only doll.

Then with one stricken look at the laughing table, she ran blindly toward the door. She wanted

to get to her own room where she could be away from everyone.

And as she ran, she heard the countess's voice.

"Poor child!" the countess exclaimed, but she too was laughing.

Bethlehem

The night is cold, and growing colder,
But they are in shelter now,
And the donkey droops its muzzle to her shoulder
And the cattle open sleepy, kindly eyes
As if to wonder
Why in the depths of night
There should be light.
Something strange is happening.
Quietly the animals ponder
The stirrings and low voices,
The silence, and then, at last, the sound
Of murmurous lullabies.

3 *The Scarlet Jacket*

AFTER Christmas in Cairo, the family started up the Nile in one of the old-fashioned white steamers which made the trip. It was a wonderful steamer, the children thought. All the cabins opened on the decks, with slatted doors which let in the air even when closed. Amidships there was a wide deck space with many easy chairs where tea was served in the middle of the afternoon, but Bob and Bess especially loved to face the steamer's stern, overlooking the river from a bench which they alone seemed to have discovered.

The Nile was copper-colored, and at sunset its

smooth surface had a pink glow across the copper. There were villages along its banks, low mud houses under palm trees, with sometimes a minaret or two. The fields were bright green with new wheat. Along the banks they could see women in straight black robes bringing down their pitchers for water, with little children often wearing just a shirt and fez. The men worked at the shadoofs, lifting the water in dripping buckets of skin, stage by stage, into the reservoirs above the fields.

"It almost never rains in Egypt," Ali, the dragoman, explained to them. "The Nile, it is the rain of Egypt."

For some reason Ali and Bess became great friends. She taught him to play casino, a simple card game her family liked, and he gave her a mummied cat from long ago. Bess loved it but Bob said it smelled, and perhaps it did.

One morning after breakfast the children realized that the steamer wasn't moving up the river as usual. It was tied by the shore, which was swarming with donkey boys in long tight robes and little caps, and furry-cheeked donkeys with strings of blue lucky beads about their necks. Ali, with a long whip, hurried down among them, ordering the boys with the poorer donkeys to go away.

Then one of the passengers went ashore, and instantly three or four boys rushed upon him, pointing to their donkeys, each shouting and claiming in broken English that his donkey was the most beautiful, the strongest, and the fastest. At that, Ali darted here and there, using his whip, and then everyone else went ashore too and was safely mounted, except Bess.

In this uproar Bess was helpless. Bewildered, she had pulled her hand loose from Mama's and now she couldn't even answer her family's calls to come down, that everything was all right, but stood at the top of the gangplank looking desperate.

Fortunately, after only a moment or two, before Papa could even get out of the saddle, the ever-present Ali swooped upon her.

"See, I have saved the best of all for you!" he

cried. "It is a jewel of a donkey for your first ride in Egypt!"

The donkey *was* a beauty. Cream-colored with black markings, it trotted as though it were dancing. Its saddle was new, its blue beads very large and bright, and its boy had fastened flowers in its bridle beneath its two long ears.

Bess had never ridden before, but she was not afraid. The donkey boy ran beside the donkey, telling it whenever there was an uneven place in the road. In front of her, beside her, behind her, poured the other donkeys with their riders and their boys. The riders were laughing, the boys were shouting, the little donkeys trotted faster and faster, while shepherds coming toward them down the road hurried to get their flocks out of the way before the cavalcade should be upon them.

Faster and still faster went the donkeys. The native policeman on a camel who acted as their guard and was supposed to lead the procession motioned to the riders to pull in their mounts.

"Galloping donkeys not allowed! Ladies and

29

gentlemen! Galloping donkeys not allowed!" shouted Ali, galloping his own donkey up and down the line of riders as he shouted.

But the donkey boys knew what the passengers liked, and what would make them give a larger baksheesh when the ride was over.

So they shouted to the donkeys and all the donkeys galloped and the riders swept on, laughing and shouting to one another, right up to the camel's heels and past them too.

Before she knew it, Bess was near the lead, with only Bob ahead. And her donkey was bigger than Bob's, and Bess was smaller than Bob, for after all she was younger. And her donkey boy was running like the wind and shouting, and Bess's donkey was galloping wildly, and Bob was looking over his shoulder and kicking his heels into his donkey to make it go faster. But it was no use. Ali really *had* saved the best donkey for Bess. And with all the grownups pounding along behind, still laughing and shouting, Bess overtook Bob and rode past him. She was the head of the whole procession, and she was wearing her new scarlet jacket with the patent leather belt, her pride and joy. Her heart was beating fast and her cheeks were red with excitement as she galloped right into Egypt. It was bright green with a red road, and it had a woman in black chasing two goats out of Bess's way and laughing too. There was a distant temple in it and a blue sky, heavy and bright, and it was all hers.

Then suddenly, without the slightest warning, the jewel of a donkey stumbled and Bess flew over its head and landed in a heap, and Bob rode up and flashed out of his saddle to her rescue, and the grownups appeared and asked if she were hurt, and the guard on his camel and Ali, too, gathered about her.

Mama was off her own donkey, brushing Bess's dress and scarlet jacket and handing her a handkerchief, for Bess was crying. She was crying too hard to tell them that she wasn't frightened or hurt. She was crying because her wonderful gallop into Egypt was over. It had been too beautiful to

last. Then Ali began to beat the donkey boy for letting the donkey stumble, and the boy began whacking the donkey for stumbling, and Bess had to stop them both. When the commotion died down, Papa lifted her back into the saddle.

"Don't you think it would be a good plan to fasten her jacket belt around the horn?" Papa suggested to Mama, and Mama thought it would be much safer. Bess wanted to protest, but she could find no words, and before them all, Papa buckled the patent leather belt around both Bess and the saddle horn. There she was in the gay scarlet jacket of which she had been so proud, tied to her saddle —she who had led the way into Egypt.

"Now that will be better," said Papa, stepping astride his own beast again, for his legs were so long that his feet almost touched the ground on each side of his donkey as he rode. And off the procession went again, more slowly.

Gone was that first wild morning joy. Bess's donkey jogged along, crowded by other donkeys. The flowers hung wilted from its bridle, the donkey boy no longer raced shouting by its side.

Egypt seemed far away, not beautiful at all. And Bess rode, staring straight ahead, sitting bolt upright in her scarlet jacket with its belt tied to the saddlebow, a figure of fun for all to see, and imagining Grandma's voice saying when she was told, as she would be told, what had happened, "Yes, Bess. Always remember, 'Pride goes before a fall.'"

To Ride into Egypt

To ride into Egypt
On a donkey,
To ride into magic,
To ride into another world,
To the music of little galloping hoofs
While the blue beads shine,
And the flowers loosen from the bridle,
And the donkey boy's running feet send up
Butterflies of dust from the road—
Oh, to ride into Egypt
In a scarlet jacket
Is to ride straight into happiness
And to be a part of it forever.

1416627

4 *Croc*

A crocodile
Grins in the Nile
Ready to eat you
After a while.

Bob made up the rhyme just *as* a rhyme at first, but Bess was such a believing child that it was not long before he enlarged Croc into an especial horror for her benefit.

"His name is Croc," explained Bob as they sat alone together on the bench at the stern of the steamer, watching the slow brown wake widen

36

and widen till it rippled along the muddy banks, "and he's mine."

"How is he yours?" Bess asked.

"Oh, I found a charm on the walls of one of the temples, and I tried it at the other side of the boat yesterday when Grandma was reading to you about the Flood. Suddenly, up came this big old croc alongside the boat—like a log, you know, but warty. And he kind of grinned at me and said, 'What is your will, O Master?' "

"Ali says there aren't any crocodiles below the cataracts any more," Bess argued uneasily.

Bob smiled.

"Well, you and Ali can believe that if you want to. I'm only telling you what I *saw*. He was about twice as long as Papa, and nearly half of him seemed to be mouth, jammed full of teeth, and he will obey anything I say. He has to. If I told him to come right up here on deck and grab you, he'd do it, like a wink."

"You're telling a story!" cried Bess, but she looked behind her. "I'm going to sit with Mama."

Every day the tales about Croc increased. Often

37

Bess, fascinated like a bird before a snake, asked for the stories herself. When the sun was bright and she could hurry off to the grownups, she only half believed them. It was exciting to sit there with her eyes on the banks of the Nile, listening to some new adventure of Croc's.

"You know he's ever and ever so old," Bob would say. "He was *the* crocodile at Kam Ombos. We haven't come to that temple yet, but they worshiped crocodiles there. He had gold earrings and a necklace of gold and lived in a marble tank, and the priests fed him every morning. But one day he got tired of being a sacred crocodile and slithered out of the sacred tank and started creepy crawly, creepy crawly, creepy crawly for the Nile."

Bob's voice had grown very creepy crawly itself, and Bess broke in: "What did the priests do?"

"Oh, they ran out and brought him wonderful offerings and heaps of the food he liked best, but he went on creepy crawly, creepy crawly—"

"*Please*, don't keep on saying 'creepy crawly,'" Bess begged.

38

"Oh, all right, then. He went right past them and slithered into the Nile, gold earrings and gold necklace and all. He was still wearing them the other day when I saw him."

"What does Croc do all the time?"

Bob was never at a loss.

"He has wonderful adventures! He was great friends with the sacred cats of Bubastis, and when-

ever they wanted to cross the Nile to go hunting mice on the other side he took them. The chief cat sat on Croc's head, right between his eyes, and the next to the chief cat sat next, and the next next, and so on. He could take forty cats at a time."

"Weren't they afraid?"

"No," Bob declared. "Not even after the time when the littlest cat told such a funny story that Croc nearly died laughing and shook so that he spilled all the cats off his back, and they were laughing so hard themselves that they nearly got drowned, but they all got ashore, somehow. After that, the chief cat made it a rule that no one should tell funny stories while they were crossing the river."

Another day Bob told about Croc's other friend, the hawk at Edfu.

"See that hawk over the river now? He's probably going to tell Croc a secret. The hawks still tell Croc everything that happens in the air and the cats tell him everything that happens on land, and of course he *knows* everything that happens in

40

the water. So he's the wisest animal that ever lived."

"Then why does he have to obey you?" Bess inquired.

"Because I know the charm," Bob declared and went off whistling.

The darker side of Croc's history was kept for bedtime. After Mama had heard their prayers and kissed them good night and the cabin was dark and the grown-up people's voices from the deck came faint and far away, and the water slithered and gurgled against the steamer's sides, and the woodwork gave low creaks and sudden rappings— then, oh, then was the hour of Croc the Horrible.

"Bess," Bob's voice would come like a hiss from the upper berth.

"Yes," poor Bess would answer from the berth below, beginning to tremble.

"Can you hear him?" They always whispered when they talked at night. Everyone seemed to whisper in the dark.

Bess would strain her ears. That sliding sound,

that rattle! In a whisper, thin and scared, she would answer, "Yes."

"He's under your berth," Bob's voice would drift down through the darkness. "But I've told him not to bite you. At least if you do as I say. Will you obey me all tomorrow? And give me that green pencil with the eraser?"

"Oh, yes!"

Something enormous and scaly was moving under Bess's berth. She could hear the rub of its heavy body, the clatter of its claws. She drew herself up into a forlorn little bunch against the wall and covered her head with the bedclothes. But well she knew that those great jaws would not be stopped by bedclothes! And through them Bob's voice, raised a little, still reached her.

"Are you listening? You'd better answer when I ask you a question. Did I tell you what Croc eats?"

"No," whimpered Bess.

"I can't hear you. Did you say yes or no?"

"No." This time a little louder.

42

"Well, he eats one girl a year. Someone fat and tender. Never a boy. He's had his eye on you, but so far my charms have kept him off you. I say those charms every morning and evening."

"Oh, thank you, Bob!" squeaked poor Bess.

One evening after the children had been put to bed, Bess made a frantic request to be allowed to sleep in the upper berth and let Bob have the lower one.

"But why, darling?" Mama asked. "Aren't you comfortable?"

Bess, though a coward, was very honorable. She never tattled. Even now the idea didn't occur to her to tell Mama about Croc.

"I've never slept up there," she whimpered. "I'd like to see what it's like."

Mama considered this, but decided against it.

"You'd fall out," she said. "You're better off where you are."

She leaned over to kiss Bess, and two warm desperate arms closed round her neck, pulling her down. Bess felt Mama's gold watch chain against her cheek, and the crisp white cotton of her shirt-waist. Then Mama pulled herself free with a little laugh.

> "Kiss me quick
> And let me go
> And do not muss
> My ruffles so!"

She stood on tiptoe to kiss Bob. The door closed as she went out.

"Bess," Bob began.

"Yes," said Bess.

"It wouldn't have made any difference. Croc would never touch me, because I'm the Master of the Charm. But he could come right out and stand up on his tail and hind legs and lick you out, even out of the top berth, as easy as pie."

"Yes," shuddered Bess.

There was no safe place for her in all the world.

The steamer remained tied up at Luxor for some days. There were wonderful things to be seen there. The temple of Luxor rose just a stone's throw down the river from the steamer's berth, and the passengers strolled off to see it at all times of day. Grandma would bring the Bible there, and she and Bess would find a good block of fallen wall and sit in the midst of the great columns, reading about Vashti or Ruth, King David or King Solomon, and Bess imagined that all temples were exactly like the temple of Luxor. But she liked best the stories about Moses as a little baby in his floating basket, and how he was found by the Egyptian princess among the reeds by the river. Bess knew from the figures on the wall just how Pharaoh's daughter must have looked, all in white, with a gold serpent twisted around her hair and necklaces of blue and gold about her throat. But Grandma went on reading, and the rest of the story got scarier and scarier. Bess couldn't bear the parts about the rod which turned into a serpent, for it made her think of Croc. She would jump up from her seat and walk up and down in front of Grandma in her black silk dress, exclaiming as she walked, "Oh, this is too exciting! This is *too* exciting!"

But even in the most exciting moments, she

never walked very far from Grandma, for Bob had told her that Croc was fond of taking his naps in the temple of Luxor.

One evening at dinner there was much talk of the moon. It was to be full that night, and a good many people thought they would walk down to see the temple by moonlight. Papa and Mama said that for once the children might stay up till nine, and as soon as it was dark they started, Bess wearing her scarlet jacket, for it was chilly. Bess walked between Papa and Mama, holding their hands and feeling reasonably safe. Moonlight makes everything look strange. The shadows don't seem to be in the right places and there are too many of them. Besides, Bob had whispered to Bess that Croc intended to come along—"out of sight, of course."

But even Croc's presence, which haunted all her days and nights anyhow, could not keep Bess from being happy in that moonlight. Most of the people from the boat looked about for a little while and then went back to the lighted decks, but Grandma and Papa and Mama and Bob and Bess and Croc lingered. The scars of the centuries faded away in the darkness. Only the beauty remained.

At last Grandma said, "Really, those children ought to be in bed," and Papa drew his watch from his vest pocket and looked at it and said, "Yes, they really ought to be," and Mama said, "I suppose so," and Bob said, "Not just yet," and Bess said, "Do we *have* to go back?" and Croc said nothing, and all six of them slowly began walking toward the lighted steamer.

But they walked slowly, for somewhere a man's voice was singing a tune perhaps as old as the pyramids, and even Bess forgot the present, forgot her fears, forgot Croc, and walked along in a sleepy dream.

At the gangplank they paused to speak to Ali, the dragoman, who was standing there looking at the moon. Mama was asking what the song was about, Bob had already run aboard, and Grandma had followed. But Bess stayed with Papa and Mama. She had forgotten to be afraid. She was looking at the moon. She was listening to the song. And listening, she stepped right off the corner of

48

the gangplank and disappeared into the river below, with a bloodcurdling yell.

She had scarcely time to remember Croc as she took one swallow of Nile water, before she was standing dripping on the bank, fished out by her friend, Ali.

At her scream the passengers came running. Now they stood along the rail, staring at Bess standing shivering in a puddle of moonlit water, her hair in strings.

"Did you slip, darling?" Mama asked anxiously. "What happened?"

The moonlight shone on all those faces which lined the rail.

"No," snuffled Bess bravely. "I just stepped in the wrong place."

"What a funny little girl she is," one face remarked to another. "But I'm glad she wasn't hurt."

Still they didn't go away. They all waited, having nothing better to do, while Mama led Bess through their midst. Wherever she stepped, her

49

shoes squdged out Nile water, and when she stood still for a moment, a new puddle formed about her feet. Her scarlet jacket was a ruin. Her dress clung to her small fat form. She looked ridiculous and she knew it. At that shameful moment Bess would have given everything she had in the world to have sunk right through the deck—yes, even if it had been straight into the waiting jaws of Croc.

The Nile

In the tall reeds of the Nile
Hides the waiting crocodile,

Ibises as white as snow
Dream above the copper flow,

Now a mirrored palm tree floats
Tangled among passing boats,

Or a swallow dips by bars
Where girls fill their water jars.

Every green and growing thing,
Every flower, every wing,

Man and child, and roof and tower
Owe existence to your power,

Mighty and exultant river,
Egypt's master, the Life-giver!

5 *The Desert People*

THE STEAMER went no farther than Assuan, where
the river came rushing down in cataracts past
rocks as smooth and wet as the backs of giant
hippopotami. Papa hired a carriage to drive out
to the quarries from which the ancient Egyptians
had cut their statues and blocks of limestone.
Grandma went along, holding her little black fold-
ing sunshade over her black bonnet with the jet
flowers on it. Bess sat between Grandma and
Mama, while Papa and Bob sat on the opposite
seat with their backs to the driver.

They had to go slowly through the town amid

cries from the driver warning people that they were coming, and cries from the people asking why they should be in such a hurry. Soon there were peddlers running beside the carriage, holding out scarves and leatherwork, old weapons and baskets. At first Papa paid no attention to them, but after a while he turned about and poked the driver in the ribs, and the driver pulled in the thin old horses, which were glad to stop. As soon as the carriage stopped, the peddlers gathered thick as buzzing flies about a piece of candy, all shouting at once.

After some bargaining, Papa bought Mama a black scarf patterned in metallic silver. And then Papa could not resist buying a basket for himself which was woven about a gourd. It was older than the others and was not at all brightly colored. It was a water basket. The woven neck, as well as the gourd, would hold water without leaking. Papa was as much pleased with it as Mama was with her silver scarf. Grandma shook her head. "Keep away!" she said sharply to the peddlers. "I don't want any of your things."

Of course Bess would have loved a scarf and Bob longed for a dagger with a silver handle, but Papa did not suggest giving them such fine presents. Instead, Bob was allowed to hold the basket and Bess the scarf as they drove on past the shops and into the open country.

But before they knew it, they were again in the midst of life. This time it was an encampment of the desert people. Papa, very much interested, again poked the driver, who willingly pulled in the horses. As the carriage slowed down, the nomad women and children gathered about it, but the men stood back near their camel's-hair tents. Papa seemed to know about these people.

"See, children," he said, "they look just like the figures on the walls of the temples."

And when he had said that, Bess saw that they did. They were very dark and their hair was braided into dozens of small braids lying along their faces and necks. Their rough clothing was torn by thorns, their legs were scarred. But the young women were like the queens in the temples,

54

with narrow noses and fine lips and big dark eyes, very bright and oval. When they smiled, their teeth were white and even, and they moved gracefully. As Bess watched a girl run back to the tents, she caught her breath. It was like seeing a greyhound run. They were all thin and swift-looking, men and women, young and old.

"Every year," Papa said, "they make the journey from the Red Sea to the Nile, across the great desert, following the almost forgotten trade routes of the ancients. They can run like antelopes and live for days on a handful of grain. They've just arrived to trade with the people of Assuan. We're lucky to see them."

Was it because Bess was inclined to be plump and loved to eat desserts and soon got out of breath when she ran, that she admired the desert people so much? Or was it because they were wild and unafraid, and she was obedient and easily frightened? Or was it because they *did* look like the people she had been seeing on the temple walls?

Anyway, Bess gazed and gazed admiringly. Bob didn't seem much impressed and watched from the carriage. Grandma, too, wouldn't move, and Mama decided to stay with her, but Papa was delighted with everything he saw and walked all about the encampment, with Bess at first hanging on to his hand. The women and children followed

them, laughing and talking to one another. Grown
more daring, they felt Bess's clothes and even knelt
to look carefully at her shoes. A girl held up Bess's
little pink hand, never hardened by work, while
the others exclaimed over it in wonder. The skinny
dogs slunk out of their way. The men watched
like hawks, proud and motionless, seeing every-

thing but never stirring. There were a few dusty camels behind the tents, and a camel's colt which the children let Bess pet. The mother camel made a growling noise, but a girl slapped its big ugly head, and everyone laughed.

For Bess it was like having wild animals for playmates. The nomad children brought her camel's milk in a gourd, but she shook her head. Then they brought her a coconut with two holes in it, and she drank its milk and was refreshed, though it felt hairy as a monkey between her hands.

At last Papa called her, and Bess trotted obediently back to the carriage. Once more she sat between Grandma and Mama, and Papa joined Bob, and the driver yelled and cracked his whip, and the old horses trotted off. The sand poured back from the moving wheels, the desert children ran beside them for a little while, and then they were alone once more on their way to the quarries.

"You know," said Papa, "I believe that basket I bought at Assuan came from this encampment. Here, Bob, hand it over and let me look at it again."

Bob handed it over, and seeing the basket put Mama in mind of the present Papa had just given her.

"I'd better take my scarf, Bess," she said. "Your hands are so hot you'll tarnish the silver."

"It isn't here," Bess wailed, after desperately hunting for the scarf all around her.

"It must be," Mama insisted.

The black and silver scarf wasn't in the carriage. Grandma remembered that Bess had been carrying it when she went off, and so did Papa. Bob, who stood by Bess in difficulties with the grownups, said he hadn't seen her with it, but everyone else had, and Bess, with a horrid sinking of the heart, remembered the feel of its heavy folds in her hands as she trotted along over the sand of the encampment.

The three grownups stared at her accusingly.

"There's no use going back," Papa declared. "There's as much chance of finding that scarf now as a minnow in the Nile. We might as well drive on to the quarries."

59

"You must have dropped it," Mama sighed. "I don't see how you could be so careless with my beautiful new scarf!"

"Children nowadays don't take any care of things, their own or other people's. Look what happened to her nice red jacket at Luxor," Grandma chimed in severely.

So many scoldings were too much for Bess's self-control, and suddenly, in the middle of them all, she burst into loud sobs, and everyone turned to stare at her in astonishment, even the driver in his fez and dusty coat, while the horses dropped into a walk, taking advantage of the interlude.

Is Far More

A ruined temple
In the sun
Is more than pillars,
Is far more
  Than pillars
  And a broken floor,
  Than a painted wall
  And an empty door—
A ruined temple
Is far more.

A ruined temple
In the sun
Is a presence,
And a voiceless speech,
  A presence
  Speaking unto each,
  A spent wave
  On a timeless beach—
A ruined temple
Sighs to each.

6 *Bess and the Sphinx*

FROM Assuan the family returned to Cairo by train. There were many things to be seen there, too many, Bess sometimes thought. The mosques were enormous and the narrow crowded streets frightened her. It was very comforting to take firm hold of Mama's blue alpaca skirt and allow herself to be dragged along, past souks and houses with overhanging balconies, carved and shuttered, where sat the women, seeing but not seen, past tiled fountains where the water carriers filled their skins, past Coptic churches and Mohammedan mosques.

62

More than once they went to the Cairo Museum, and looking at the beautiful things of ancient Egypt which had been found in the earth or in the tombs, the entire family became filled with a longing to find something themselves, however small and unimportant. In a few days they were planning to travel to Hamburg and would sail for home on a German liner across the wintry Atlantic. Their trip abroad was almost at an end. How wonderful, they all said, if they could carry back some little treasure which they had discovered for themselves!

Bess did not understand a great deal about the ancient Egyptians, but from resting her chin on endless glass cases she knew well enough what common objects were to be found. There were the scarabs, the winged beetles which represented the sun and which the ancient Egyptians made in stone or pottery. There were little figures of Osiris, god of the dead, found in every tomb, some still turquoise blue and some which had lost their enamel, gray with the rub of centuries. Then there were blue beads or others of jade or carnelian, used in necklaces. Bess stared at these things solemnly, but, knowing that she seldom could find even a clean handkerchief in a bureau drawer, she had little hope that she would be the one to make any discovery that might be made.

"I bet I'll find something," Bob boasted. "If all these bushels and bushels of things were found by people, why shouldn't I find just one?"

"I bet you will," agreed Bess, edging away from a mummy case, whose painted face appeared to be staring at her too fixedly.

Papa had saved the most famous trip for the last. That was the trip to the Pyramids. After breakfast, they took a carriage and drove out to the village of Giza among its palms, with the desert sands lying fierce and shifting as far as eye could reach.

Under the coconut palms the Bedouins waited with camels and donkeys and even one or two carriages with very broad wheels which would not bury themselves too deeply in the sand. Grandma and Mama took a carriage. Papa chose a donkey, and Bob of course wanted a camel. If there had been an elephant, he would have wanted the elephant, for he was an adventurous boy.

Bess waited undecided. She saw Bob mount onto the kneeling camel's saddle and heard the animal gurgling and grumbling as it rose pitching to its feet. There was a shout from Bob.

"It's wonderful, Bess! If you don't take a camel you're a fraidycat!"

A camel man and several donkey boys were urging their mounts upon her. Bess looked longingly at the small, safe, furry donkeys.

"You'd better try something new, Bess," Papa said. "This is your last chance. Take a camel."

Trembling, Bess allowed herself to be led to a camel. It was lying down, but even so, its saddle seemed very high in the air. She scrambled up, but alas! as she scrambled, panting, the camel turned its head and growled at her, a cross, ready-to-bite growl. She saw its large eye and its long yellow teeth close to her plump, black-stockinged leg, and with a howl flung herself upward into the saddle while the Bedouin yanked the camel's head back where it belonged. A sort of earthquake fol-

65

lowed as the creature got to its feet, and then off
the procession started, carriage, camels, and
donkey.

After a little while, Bess began almost to enjoy
riding a camel. Ahead she could see the three
great triangles of the Pyramids against the deep
blue sky, and near them rose the battered face
of the Sphinx, with the sand drifting between its
paws.

Grandma had read to her about the flight into
Egypt. And Mama said that there was a legend
that the Holy Family camped near the Sphinx and

66

that while Joseph watched by the campfire, Mary and the Babe had slept, pillowed in the shelter of the Sphinx's paws. It made the Sphinx seem a friendly sort of thing.

Bess thought about this as she slowly bobbed along, holding on tight and keeping a sharp eye on the camel's head to make sure it didn't try to bite her again. She made up a poem:

> Pyramids are all right,
> But the Sphinx
> Thinks and thinks and
> Thinks and thinks.

She liked her poem at first, but after a while she thought there were too many "thinks" and changed it to:

> Pyramids are grand,
> But the Sphinx
> Sits in the sand
> And thinks and thinks.

She didn't repeat her poem to anyone because people always smiled at her poems. Bess liked the

Sphinx a lot. The Pyramids were too scary. She refused to be pulled up their enormous blocks with Papa and Bob to see the view, and when they, with Mama, followed a guide down the long dark inner passage to see the tomb of the Pharaoh, she stayed in the shadow of the Sphinx near Grandma, who remained seated under her sunshade in the carriage.

The Sphinx was different. It had a face, enormous as it was, and a sad look, staring off into the distance forever and forever and forever.

"Don't look so lonesome, Sphinx," Bess said to it, patting its huge side with her small hand.

It was pleasant there in the shadow of the Sphinx.

"The Sphinx and I are friends," Bess thought. She hadn't had this feeling anywhere else in Egypt, as though a great something was aware of her, and felt kindly, too.

Now Bob was back interrupting her thoughts, telling her about the tomb in the pyramid. "It's the most exciting thing we've done in Egypt, Bess. You've missed the best. You've missed the best

twice. I don't know whether the *very* best was climbing right up to the top, or going *into* the pyramid, but either way you've missed the best thing in Egypt."

"The Sphinx is the best," said Bess.

"Silly!" said Bob. "What can you *do* with your old Sphinx except *look* at it?"

Bess couldn't answer, but she knew she was right. Now the family, except for Grandma, went off on foot to examine some of the ruins of temples and smaller tombs. They were a very thorough family. Bess trudged along a little behind the others. At every step her feet sank down into the soft sand. Walking was hard, and she began to think that a good grip on Mama's skirt would help a lot, when the toe of her scuffed shoe hit against something.

For a wonder, Bess looked down to see what it was. At first it seemed just like a stone she had kicked against. But it was more than a stone. Gray as the sand, worn by the sand, there lay a little clay figure of Osiris, such as she had seen in the museum, with its arms crossed in the magic way upon its breast. It was hers, her own, not bought, but found, the gift of the Sphinx! There it lay, her own.

If Bess had been a Pharaoh, she would have added another inscription to those in honor of the Sphinx, like the many inscriptions in the temples which had been read to her.

"I, Bess," her inscription would have read, "beloved of the Sphinx, after many misadventures and defeats, have come into victory. They said, 'Ha! She never will find anything!' They declared, 'Ho! She doesn't know her right hand from her left!' They exclaimed, 'Silly! She wouldn't recognize a treasure if she saw it!' But the Sphinx opened my eyes. It placed the figure of Osiris before my feet. It gave the treasure into my hand. Let me hereafter be called Bess the Victorious, Bess the Discoverer, Bess the Great."

And unable to contain her joy, Bess gave a skip, which at the time nobody noticed.

And the Pyramids Stand

Here the sun and the centuries lie heavy.
Egypt is old, old, old.
The painted temples stand where they have always stood,
And in the hidden tombs the Pharaohs lie
With their treasures of gold.

The sun and the centuries lie heavy,
And the Sphinx stares, as always, across the sand.
Nothing has ever changed that calm and level gaze.
The past is the present, while the Sphinx
And the Pyramids stand.

7 *I'll Never Reach New York*

IT WAS time now to say good-bye to Egypt, and the Nile, and the palms, and the camels, and the Sphinx, and the princesses, who Bess knew were now only to be found on the temple walls. Papa had their tickets on a German liner in his billfold.

"It will be a winter crossing," Papa said, "and the North Atlantic can be very rough then. I thought we'd better take one of the biggest liners afloat."

They had had one rough day when they came over in May, at least Grandma had called it rough, and the children hadn't minded it at all. So cheer-

74

fully they traveled to Hamburg, first across the Mediterranean, then through Europe, which was increasingly cold and deep in snow. There were no art galleries now, and no wanderings under the trees from one medicinal spring to another, nor rosy clouds seen from a peak of the Alps.

Egypt with its sands and donkeys and temples seemed like a dream, and Bess clutched the little Osiris which she carried in her pocket in a padded bag that Grandma had made for it. Only so did the wonder of that day come back to her, and she could see again the camels and Papa's donkey and Grandma's pair of old horses resting in the shade of the Sphinx, and feel again the triumph of her discovery. She was counting the days until she could show her treasure to the children at school.

But first they must cross the North Atlantic in February. That seemed easy in this great liner! It was like a palace, all lights and gilding on the paneled walls, and fine furniture and deep carpets on the floors. There were salons and dining rooms, writing rooms, a library, a smoking room for the men, and a drawing room for the ladies.

For dinner that first night Mama put on her prettiest dress to match her forget-me-not blue eyes, and Grandma wore her lavender dotted swiss with a V of lace at the neck, and Papa said he was sorry he hadn't brought anything suitable, and Bob, under protest, appeared in a white Peter Thompson sailor suit with a bos'n's whistle on a blue cord around his neck, and Bess wore her flowered challis with puffed sleeves and black velvet trimming. They all had a nice time, and after dinner listened to the orchestra and watched the other passengers walk by, but there weren't any children Bob's and Bess's age.

That was the last time most of the passengers saw the dining room for many a long day. During the night the liner sailed into the stormy North Atlantic and began to pitch and toss and roll and wiggle like a thing possessed. All night Bess clung to the side of her berth so as not to fall out and listened to Grandma groan from across the stateroom. In the morning Papa, looking green, stopped in for a moment from the next stateroom to see if they were all right, but only Bob was all right.

Only Bob got up at all. Even Papa went back to his berth. All that day the stewards carried trays to people's staterooms and carried them back again with almost nothing eaten.

"In the dining room they have racks on the tables to keep the dishes from sliding," reported Bob, and off he went in search of further marvels.

The liner groaned and creaked, straining this way and that. On the third day the ceilings of all the palatial salons began to leak. Salt water dripped down on satin sofas and deep carpets. Bob reported that the only dry place on the ship was the smoking room, and here the few hardy passengers who were still on their feet gathered to talk about the bad trips they had known or heard of.

When the ceiling over Bob's top bunk began to leak, Papa stuffed the crack with one of his night-shirts. Papa could still take care of his family when he had to, but Mama and Grandma and Bess could scarcely lift their heads, lost in a misery that seemed to go on forever.

Now Bob reported that the doors to the decks

were barred, for the storm had washed away the rails, and the sailors went about their duties hanging on to emergency ropes.

One especially awful night, the woman in the stateroom across from Bess's began to scream that the ship was going down, until her husband quieted her. Already the liner was overdue in New York. It was so sheathed in ice that it moved more and more sluggishly and was less and less able to climb above the endless attack of the waves.

Then one morning Bess woke up feeling a little better. She was dizzy and miserable, but she was better. She felt the Osiris in its padded bag under her pillow.

"I'm going to get up," she told Grandma. Bob had already gone to breakfast, and Bess had the cabin floor space to herself, but even so she got dressed the hard way, flung from one side of the stateroom to the other, once barely getting out of the way of Grandma's steamer trunk, which sprang at her from under a bunk like a dog out of its kennel. But finally Bess had her clothes on, and Grandma nodded approval. She liked to see anyone make an effort, even though she couldn't do it herself. She helped Bess to brush her straight hair.

"You don't look like much," she said, "but nobody will notice."

Bess knocked at Mama's and Papa's stateroom door.

"You're getting *up*?" exclaimed Mama and shut her eyes.

"Good girl," said Papa and shut his eyes too.

Bess found the dining room with only a handful of people in it. They all spoke to her as if she were a castaway coming out of the breakers onto an island where they were already camping. She was one of them, even if only for a little while.

Bess ate something, but she couldn't get much down. With Osiris for company, she went to the smoking room and there she found Bob. He was glad to see her. "Good old blunderbuss," he said, "now you can slide with me."

It was really fun for a while. They sat down together on the floor. One wave would slide them across the room. Then Bob showed Bess how to turn in time for the next wave to slide them back to the other side. Back and forth they went, back and forth, until some of the few passengers began to look rather sick.

"Come here, children," called an old gentleman. "I'll teach you a rhyme." Bob said, "I have to learn rhymes in school," and went on sliding, but Bess was ready to stop.

She sat down in a chair next to the old gentleman (all the chairs were fastened to the floor so they didn't move), and he taught her a rhyme.

Oh, Mr. Captain, stop the ship.
I want to get off and walk!
I feel so flippity floppity flip
I'll never reach New York!

Later Bess tried to teach her rhyme to Papa and Mama and Grandma, but somehow they didn't want to hear it. Only Osiris was really interested. And she said it over and over to him in a low voice when she went back to bed, which was pretty soon after talking to the old gentleman.

But the next day was really much smoother, and everyone began to come out of their staterooms like bedraggled bees out of a broken honeycomb.

Next morning the liner would dock, and the news gave the passengers courage. At the captain's dinner that night, scarcely a seat was empty, and the wooden racks were no longer needed to keep the dishes in place.

All Bess's family was gathered about the same small table at which they had eaten on the first night. They were wearing their best clothes again, and if they looked a little rumpled and woebegone, so did most of the other people. But voices were cheerful again and color was coming back to pale cheeks. Papa made jokes with a straight face and Mama laughed at them. Grandma sat upright and solid, keeping an eye on the children's manners, while Bob and Bess giggled at Papa's jokes and at their own.

But at last the main courses were over and the stewards began to bring in the desserts. There were ice cream castles with steep colored roofs and high turrets. There were swans on glassy lakes, and an American eagle. But for their table appeared the nicest dessert of all, or so Bess thought. It was a tall, pretty Red Ridinghood, with

a face and dress of vanilla ice cream and a cloak and hood of strawberry ice. Over one arm she carried a chocolate basket, and the other hand rested on the head of a big brown wolf with white teeth, as fierce looking as any wolf in a fairy tale.

Papa looked at Bess's excited face and asked her, quite out of turn, "What will you have, Bess?"

"I'll take the wolf, thank you, Papa," said Bess, all in one breath. And very lightly she touched the Osiris in her pocket.

"Look out, it'll bite you!" cried Bob. "See those teeth!"

But Bess and Osiris were beyond his reach.

"Silly," she said. "He's my wolf. He might bite *you* if I told him to, but he won't bite me. I know the right charm."

Bob's mouth opened to say something, and then, catching Bess's eye, he grinned at her instead. And Bess smiled back at him, sedately.

Hunt

The wind is a rider,
Furiously he rides, hallooing.
Hear him! hear him!
And hear how the waves answer
As they come on, pell-mell,
The foam slavering from their gray jaws.
They pant against the sides of the ship,
While it tosses and struggles
Trying to throw them off.
Courage, brave ship! Hold out for a little longer
And the wind will ride on with his hounds,
The wind, mad with impatience.

BESS AFTER EGYPT

—A note from Elizabeth Coatsworth—

DO I remember Bess across the years? Oh yes, very clearly. If I were a tree, Bess would be the "heartwood," as the lumbermen say, the central core which was once the sapling around which every tree grows. People count a tree's age by its rings, and can tell its history too. The wide rings mark a year of strong growth, the narrow rings tell of years of little rain or of blights. If I think of myself as a tree, then the ring which marks Bess's year abroad would be a wide, wide ring.

It was in that year that Bess discovered the excitement of travel and of foreign lands. Brought up in the safety and one-day-much-like-anotherness of family life, she suddenly was taken into new worlds, heard strange speech she couldn't understand, slept in hotels instead of in her own bed, knew the uncertain balancings of ships, was rushed along in hooting trains, and saw mountains, vineyards, and foreign cities of great beauty.

But these were only an introduction to the wonders that awaited Bess in Egypt. It was with them that her inner life perhaps began. After returning home to her old quiet life, she still dreamed at night of galloping alone and happy on a donkey into an Egypt blazing

87

with sunlight. By day she loved to be read to, and when no one would read to her she made up stories for herself, long trailing stories that might last for weeks. Did Egypt start Bess daydreaming, or did it only give color and shape to the daydreams already within her?

In those days Bess was built to sit rather than to run. If she were amused, it was deep down. She seldom laughed. Some people found her speech hard to understand, and she never could carry a tune. Seldom was there a more credulous child, and she was obedient, unless she forgot what she had been told to do. But always she was loving. Who would have guessed that within this small, solid, rather wistful form there burned a passion for travel, for the quality of places and peoples, which only waited its opportunity to appear?

Looking back across the years, I think that after Egypt, Bess was never again quite the same stay-at-home, bumbling Bess of earlier days. She was of course still Bess, but she had become aware of the world around her. Soon she would be Betty, making up rhymes before she went to sleep. And then she would be Elizabeth, who would have two passions, traveling and sitting pen in hand—as she is now, remembering Bess.

88